My Mommy

IN LOVING MEMORY OF MY MOTHER,
CATHERINE A. MAGURN,
AND IN HONOR OF MY DAUGHTER,
LISA PARADIS MACGREGOR

Library of Congress Cataloging-in-Publication Data

Paradis, Susan.

My mommy / Susan Paradis.

p. cm.

Summary: A young girl celebrates how her
mother, just like the animals that always seem near,
expresses her love through such daily activities as
eating, playing, and snuggling together.

ISBN 1-886910-73-1 (alk. paper)

[1. Mother and child-Fiction.] I. Title.

PZ7.P2128 My 2002

[E]-dc21   2002024287

MY MOMMY

SUSAN PARADIS

Front Street

ASHEVILLE, NORTH CAROLINA

My mommy

feeds me

and helps me

start the day.

She always says

I'm beautiful.

Sometimes she

says, "Surprise!"

My mommy

holds me tight

and lets me go

to keep my secrets.

If I'm lost,

she shows the way.

If I cry,

she hears me.

She makes me better

and cheers me on.

At night my mommy

washes me.

She tucks me into bed

and in the morning

tiptoes in and whispers

"Rise and shine."